Are You The Flower or The Weed?

A School Bully Learns the Pathway to Kindness

By Karen Garn, M. Ed., LPC

*****

Dedicated
to
my grandsons,
Brandon, Daniel, and Emerson,
and to
my granddaughter,
Mia

I am proud
to say
that all four have
accepted and
continue to
receive numerous school awards
for showing
kindness to others.

*****

My name is Max, and I used to rule the school – or so I thought. Before I became the school bully, I never imagined in a zillion years that I'd be the kid who spent more time in the principal's office than in my class.

I thought being mean made me so cool. But when my world started to fall apart, I realized I had a lot to learn.

I saw how the big kids got attention by being mean, so I thought I'd try it too. I started shoving kids out of line to show how tough I was. I wouldn't let them play, and I got in their faces to show them I was in charge. I'd call them names, try to trip them, and then laugh. I thought all this would make everyone notice me, and maybe I'd even become the most popular kid in school.

But I quickly learned that being mean wasn't cool at all. It wasn't the kind of attention I wanted, and it definitely did not make me popular. My friends stopped asking me to play after school and at recess. Most days, I had to eat lunch alone in the cafeteria because I was always in trouble, and I got so tired of having to do my schoolwork in the principal's office.

I had never felt so sad and alone. I started thinking about how I used to help others. I always had a smile to share with everyone, no matter who they were! I used to be the first person to tell a friend, "Good job!" And I always made sure everyone got to join in when playing a game.

I knew I needed help, and I knew just the person I could count on.

So, off I went to visit Grandma. I had just sat down when she asked, "Max, is everything okay? You look so sad; do you want to talk?" I nodded and started to tell her everything.

"I'm tired of being in trouble all the time," I admitted. She listened as I told her how I felt.

When I was done, she said, "Max, I am here for you. It's great that you want to change, but it's not going to be easy. It's going to take some hard work on your part."

The next day, Grandma took me outside to her beautiful flower garden. It was the most peaceful place, full of colorful flowers – big ones, small ones, in every color you could imagine. Just being there made me feel happy. As we walked around, Grandma said, "See those weeds growing between the flowers? Start picking them out."

I had always liked helping Grandma, but I didn't understand why she was asking me to pull weeds.

But I got down anyways and started pulling the weeds one by one. After a while, I noticed something: the weeds were getting really close to the flowers, almost like they were going to hurt them. But the flowers didn't let that happen. No matter how many weeds were around, the flowers kept growing, standing tall, and sharing their beautiful colors with the world around them.

I called Grandma over to tell her what I had figured out about the flowers and the weeds. Grandma smiled and said, "I think you may be on to something, Max. Tell me, which one are you, the flower or the weed?" I didn't know what to say. I was still thinking about those nasty weeds. Then she said, "I think this is the perfect time to tell you one of my favorite stories." She paused before asking,

"Are you the Flower or the Weed?"

The weed may invade your space
or put a finger in your face.

The flower knows it can't control
what others do or say,
but knows it can be kind to others
each and every day.

The weed may start to call you names
to try to make you feel ashamed.

The weed may talk behind your back.
You'll hear it laugh as it talks its smack.

The weed may say things that aren't true
to turn others against you too.

The flower knows it can't control
what others do or say,
but knows it can be kind to others
each and every day.

Are you the Flower or the Weed?

The weed may roll its eyes at you
just to see what you will do.

The weed may stand and wait around
just so it can stare you down.

The weed may tell you, "Go away!
You are not allowed to play."

The flower knows it can't control
what others do or say,
but knows it can be kind to others
each and every day.

Are you the Flower or the Weed?

The weed may try to trip you when
you walk by it with a friend.

The weed may push you out of line
to see if you will start to whine.

The weed may hold its fists just right
and waits to see if you will fight.

The flower knows it can't control
what others do or say,
but knows it can be kind to others
each and every day.

Are you the Flower or the Weed?

But one day, the weed's friends will not play,
so, it decides to change its ways.
It realizes what it put the flower through
and admits it wasn't the right thing to do.

But then the flower walks by.
The weed looks up, and it says, "Hi!"
As the flower starts to go,
the weed says, "I would like you to know,
I'm not the way I used to be.
Will you come and play with me?"

In the end...
The flower and the weed became the best of friends.
Before they started on their way,
they pinky promised to be kind to others every day.

Grandma asked, "So, Max, what do you think? Are you the flower or the weed?"

I thought about it for a second and said, "I get it now, Grandma. The flower is kind, which makes people happy. And the weed was mean, but it was able to change. Starting today, I'm going to be the flower," I declared.

Grandma smiled. "I'm so proud of you, Max. I knew you would figure it out."

Being kind is about doing nice things for
others without expecting anything in return.
Showing kindness can be as simple as sharing
a smile or a compliment, holding the door
for a friend, or letting a classmate go
before you in line.

So...before you close this book,
tell me...

Are you the Flower or the Weed?

 28

Kindness matters wherever you go,
you'll reap the benefits of what you sow.
Kindness matters wherever you are,
it can spread to others from afar.
Kindness matters in whatever you do,
you may even catch a smile coming back to you.

~Karen Garn

I hope you enjoyed this book as much as I loved writing it. If you did, it would mean so much to me if you could take a few minutes and leave your kind feedback as it will help other readers to discover the story too. Thank-you so much!

Made in United States
North Haven, CT
16 December 2024

62709485R00020